Curious George®

Dragon Dance

Adaptation by Adah Nuchi
Based on the TV series teleplay written by Scott Gray

Houghton Mifflin Harcourt
Boston New York

ISBN: 978-0-544-78500-7 paper-over-board
ISBN: 978-0-544-78499-4 paperback

Design by Afsoon Razavi
Cover art adaptation by Rudy Obrero and Kaci Obrero
www.hmhco.com
www.curiousgeorge.com
Manufactured in China
SCP 10 9 8 7 6 5 4 3 2 1
4500612703

It was a beautiful day. George and his friend Marco were taking a walk when all of a sudden they came across a big party in the middle of the street. They wondered what could be happening.

"Happy New Year!" a girl said to them. George and Marco were confused. New Year's happened on January first, and today wasn't January first.

"It's Chinese New Year," the girl explained. "Welcome to Chinatown! My name is Lily."

Lily told George and Marco all about Chinese New Year. The holiday is also called the Spring Festival, and it is a time for families to get together. It is the most important celebration for families in China. Today there would be fireworks and a parade. And at the very end of the parade, there would be a dragon dance.

"Do you want to see the dragon?" Lily asked. Of course they did.

The dragon was in the storeroom of Lily's parents' restaurant. This year Lily was going to lead the dragon dance with her cousins. It was a huge honor. Dragons were considered to be helpful and wise, and the dragon dance would keep away bad luck in the new year.

There was just one problem. “The parade is starting soon,” she said. “But my cousins are running late.” Lily wanted to practice the dragon dance, but there was no one to hold the middle or back of the dragon.

Then Lily had an idea. Maybe George and Marco could help her practice the dragon dance. Marco got underneath the middle of the dragon, and George went to the end.

"Just walk around and move back and forth like a dragon," Lily said.

But it's not easy being a dragon inside a storeroom. There were too many things to bump into.

George, Marco, and Lily took the dragon out on the street, where they zigged, and zagged, and zigged again.

"You need to stay behind me in a line," Lily explained.
"You also need to keep an even distance."

They were moving like a dragon! Until . . . Crash!
"Whoops!" Lily said. "It's important to keep your eyes forward, too."

When they got up, they noticed the dragon's nose was missing!

That's when George spotted the nose across the street. But not before a dog did.

By the time George, Marco, and Lily caught up with the dog, the dragon nose was completely ruined.

Luckily, George had an idea. They could make a new nose! They hurried to George's house, where he had an entire box of art supplies.

First they tried a round ball. It was close, but it didn't look enough like the old nose. George remembered that the old nose had red and gold stripes and it was curvy. Maybe he could use red and gold yarn!

They made a nose out of yarn. It was the right color,
but it was a little too droopy.

George needed to find the right material. Felt wasn't firm enough, and neither was ribbon. But pipe cleaners might work! They were strong and bendy.

The pipe cleaners looked right, but something was still missing. The rest of the dragon head was covered in red cloth. They needed the new nose to match, and they were almost out of time.

George went to the kitchen. Surely there was something there. He opened cabinets and drawers. Then he found something: red napkins!

The new nose was perfect.

"The dragon looks wonderful!" Lily said. But the parade had already started. Would they be too late?

"You said the parade ends with the dragon!" Marco said. They could still make it if they took a shortcut through the park.

The three of them raced off like a dragon. They kept their eyes forward, they stayed in a line, and they kept an even distance.

They arrived at the parade just in time! However, Lily's dad had some bad news. Lily's cousins were still stuck in traffic. They wouldn't make it to the parade. Who would help her with the dragon dance?

Lily knew a couple of dragon dance experts: George and Marco! And that's how, with a little bit of practice, and the right materials, a monkey became a dragon!

Did You Know?

CHINESE NEW YEAR is also known as Spring Festival. It marks the first day of the Chinese calendar, but the date changes each year! It always falls between the middle of January and the middle of February. There are different ways to celebrate Chinese New Year. These are some traditions people practice for the holiday:

A CLEAN HOUSE: A thoroughly cleaned house is thought to give people a fresh start for the new year.

LUCKY DECORATIONS: Red is considered a lucky color in China. Around Chinese New Year you'll see red lanterns and other decorations hanging in the street.

RED ENVELOPES: Children are often given gifts of money in red envelopes. This is also for good luck!

FIREWORKS: At midnight on Chinese New Year, cities and towns are lit up with exploding fireworks shows.

LANTERNS: The Lantern Festival is the traditional end of the celebrations. People send glowing lanterns flying into the sky or floating on the sea, rivers, or lakes.

Let's Make Fireworks Decorations!

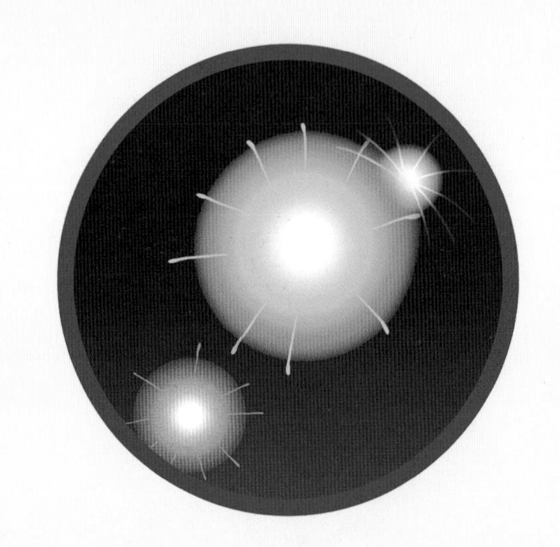

Fireworks are a fun part of the Chinese New Year celebration. Even when you can't see real fireworks, you can still decorate your home with them.

You'll need . . .

- black construction paper
- glitter
- white non-toxic glue
- old newspaper

What to do:

1. Spread the newspaper out to protect your surface from glitter.
2. Using the glue, draw fireworks on the black paper.
3. Quickly, before the glue dries, shake glitter over the glue.
4. Carefully pour the extra glitter back into the container.
5. Ask an adult to help you hang up your decorations!